As I Get Older, I Must Not Forget

Jonathan Brown

ISBN 978-1-63874-462-7 (paperback)
ISBN 978-1-63874-463-4 (digital)

Christian Faith Publishing
832 Park Avenue
Meadville, PA 16335
www.christianfaithpublishing.com

Printed in the United States of America

To my beautiful children, Jonathan Jr. and Mya.

At the start of every day, my mommy and my daddy peek their heads into my bedroom, saying, "Jonathan, don't forget to make your bed." One morning as I wake up, I think to myself...

REESE

TOYS

As I get older, I must not forget
to kneel by my bed and pray.
"Dear Father God,
Lead me with your shining light.
Help me to do what is right.
I will keep you first in all I do.
With peace, love, and joy,
I love you. Amen."

As I get older, I must
not forget to thank
God for my family.
"God, thank you for the best mommy
and daddy in the whole world."

As I get older, I must not forget to keep building
my relationship with God by going to church.
Every Sunday, my mom irons my clothes,
and my dad drives us to church.

As I get older, I must not forget to listen to
my parents and help with chores.
My favorite chore is to make sure my poodle,
named Romeo, has food and water.

As I get older, I must not forget to be kind to everyone even if they are not kind to me.

Sometimes at the park, kids call me names,
but I am still nice just the same.

As I get older, I must not forget that
God loves everyone, even you!

As I get older, I must not forget to love all people.

As I get older, I must not forget to read the
Bible and spread the Word of God.
I can share the Word of God on the bus, on
the playground, and even at day care.

19

As I get older, I must not forget to keep God first.

20

As I get older, I must not forget to be honest.
Sometimes it can be hard to tell the truth,
but God already knows the truth.

23

KINDNESS

LOVE EVERYONE

BE HONEST

As I get older, I must not forget to always try my best.
The most important things that I try my best at
are following all the teachings that my mommy
and my daddy taught me in this book.

Once I am older and have a family, I must not forget to pass this on to my children and tell them how much I love them.

About the Author

In 1988, Jonathan Brown Sr. was born in Rome, New York. He experienced major trauma as a child from abuse, being placed into group homes and foster homes. Jonathan said the only one whom he could depend on and turn to was God. He has a degree in chemical dependency and another in community human services. Jonathan has over thirteen years' experience working with all populations, ranging from children with developmental disabilities to incarcerated individuals.

Jonathan received a civilian award from the Utica, New York, chief of police in May 2010 for trying to save a young child who was ejected out of a vehicle and into a barge canal. He is a philanthropist and has a deep passion for helping those who are underprivileged and less fortunate. Jonathan wants all children to know that believing in themselves and self-empowerment can propel them to overcome any obstacle. The author states, "I was inspired to write this children's book because I want to demonstrate a level of success that anyone can obtain through Christ Jesus." This book illustrates the significance of a child being taught about God at an early age. Then he remembers to utilize the teachings in real-life experiences and pass them down to his children once he is an adult. This book is dedicated to my beautiful children, Jonathan Jr. and Mya. I thank my Lord and Savior, Jesus Christ, for all the blessings in my life. I can do all things through Christ, who strengthens me.

CPSIA information can be obtained
at www.ICGtesting.com
Printed in the USA
JSHW040623100822
29117JS00001B/1